Follow That Star

To Philippa — K.O.
For Carol, Cameron and Jeffrey — K.L.

Kids Can Press Ltd. acknowledges with appreciation the assistance of the Canada Council and the Ontario Arts Council in the production of this book.

Canadian Cataloguing in Publication Data

Oppel, Kenneth
    Follow that star

ISBN 1-55074-134-9

1. Jesus Christ - Juvenile literature. I. LaFave, Kim. II. Title.

PS8579.P64F76 1994   jC813'.54   C94-930756-4
PZ7.066Fo 1994

Text copyright © 1994 by Kenneth Oppel
Illustrations copyright © 1994 by Kim LaFave

Kids Can Press Ltd.
29 Birch Avenue
Toronto, Ontario, Canada
M4V 1E2

Edited by Debbie Rogosin
Designed and typeset by N.R.Jackson
Printed and bound in Hong Kong by
   Wing King Tong Company Limited

94 0 9 8 7 6 5 4 3 2 1

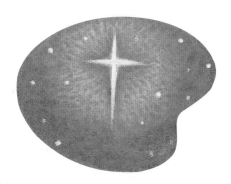

Follow That Star

Written by Kenneth Oppel

•

Illustrated by Kim LaFave

KIDS CAN PRESS LTD., TORONTO

Zach wasn't even there when the angels came.

He was down the hill, on the other side of the high thicket, grumbling and trying to count sheep in the dark.

"Worst job in the world," he muttered. "Twenty-one ... twenty-two ... long hours, low wages ... twenty-three ... twenty-four ..."

If he had looked behind him, he would have seen a halo of light around the hill, blazing like a thousand candles.

If he had stopped counting for a second and listened, he would have heard the soft music of a thousand wind chimes and oboes.

But he didn't turn around.

He didn't listen.

And he missed the angels.

When he got back to the campfire, Ben and Josh weren't there. He found a note by his blanket. It said:

We've seen angels. We're going to Bethlehem.

"Angels!" Zach exclaimed. "Lazy, that's what they are! Leaving me to do all the work. They're probably taking a nice snooze somewhere. Angels, my foot!"

He sat down against the tree and folded his arms across his chest. He humphed. He hemmed and hawed. Angels! He didn't believe in angels. *He'd* certainly never seen any.

Then Zach noticed something on the grass — something sparkly and bright, like a fine morning dew. And there it was in the branches of the trees, too, glittering like droplets of ice.

He'd heard stories about it but he'd never believed it.

"Angel mist," he whispered to himself.

Zach began to feel left out. He'd never seen angels. Ben and Josh had seen angels.

If it weren't for those stupid sheep. He looked off into the distance. Bethlehem was a long way, maybe ten or eleven miles. It was farther than he'd ever been.

Who would look after the sheep? He couldn't leave them alone. They were the stupidest sheep in the world. They'd wander off and get into trouble. And there were sheep thieves everywhere. He'd have to take the whole flock with him.

"Come on, sheep!" he called out, running down the hill. "We're going to Bethlehem!"

The night was clear and full of stars. Zach took deep breaths of the crisp, clean air. He felt happy. He was going to Bethlehem to see angels. Maybe he'd even catch up with Ben and Josh, and they could all walk together, laughing and telling stories.

It wasn't long before Zach was very cold, and very tired. He tried to keep all the sheep together, but they were slow and kept straying off the path. They tripped over one another's hooves. They bonked heads, trying to go in opposite directions. They forgot they were sheep and tried to hop like kangaroos. One of them even climbed up a tree and sat there in the branches, bleating in confusion.

"These are the stupidest sheep in the world!" Zach shouted.

Up ahead was an inn. Light
danced behind the windows,
and Zach could hear merry voices
spilling out into the night.

He went inside to get warm.

"Where are you off to?" they asked him.

"Bethlehem," he said. "Ben and Josh saw angels."

"Angels!" they exclaimed. "Don't tell us you
believe in angels. A man of your age!"

Zach's face coloured.

"Well, I think I do," he said quietly.

"It's a long walk to Bethlehem," they said. "And
it's getting cloudy. Stay here with us."

Zach nodded. He wanted to stay. It was warm
and cosy at the inn, and he was very tired. But
suddenly, the doors and windows blew open. The
room was filled with wind and a most strange and
wonderful smell.

"Angels," he said. "That could only be the smell
of angels."

He ran outside and gathered his flock. He was going to Bethlehem if it was the last thing he did. He wanted to see angels. He wondered what they looked like. He could hardly wait to find out.

Then Zach stopped and looked around.

"Oh great," he grumbled. "I'm lost."

"Hello?" said a trembly voice behind him. "Is there anyone there?"

It was a very old man, lying in the shadows at the side of the road.

"I seem to have fallen down," he said.

Zach rushed over and lifted the old man to his feet. He weighed hardly anything at all.

"Thank you very much," said the old man. "Now tell me, what's a shepherd doing on the road at this hour?"

"I'm trying to get to Bethlehem," Zach told him.

"It's going to take you a long time with all those sheep."

"I know," sighed Zach. "They're the stupidest sheep in the world. But what can I do? I've got to take care of them, and I don't want to lose any. Do you know the way to Bethlehem?"

"Why do you want to go to Bethlehem?" the old man asked.

"Angels," said Zach. "There are angels there."

"Don't be ridiculous," said the old man. "There's no such thing."

"Oh yes there is," said Zach firmly. "I saw angel mist, and when I was at the inn, the windows blew open and there was a wonderful smell and —"

The old man smiled, pointed up at the sky and said, "Follow that star."

Zach looked. Shining through a gap in the clouds was a huge, glistening star. Zach knew a thing or two about stars. He used them to find his way home in the dark. He could also tell time by the stars. And he'd never seen a star like this before.

"Thanks," said Zach, but the old man had already disappeared.

Zach followed the star through the
valley. He followed it over the next hill.
He made his way by the light of this strange
new star along the dusty, winding road, through sleeping
villages, all the way to a shallow stream.

When he got to the stream, his sheep wouldn't cross.

"I forgot," Zach moaned. "My sheep don't like water.
They're the stupidest sheep in the world."

He was never going to get to Bethlehem at this rate.

"Can I help you?" said a voice beside him.

"Who are you?" Zach asked.

"A carpenter," said the man. He wore a leather tool belt around his waist, and he led a mule carrying long pieces of wood.

"My sheep won't walk through the stream," Zach told him. "And there's no bridge in sight."

"Don't worry. We'll build a bridge," said the man. "It won't take long."

They hammered and sawed. In no time at all, Zach and the carpenter had built a little bridge across the stream.

"Thank you very much," said Zach. "Maybe I'll make it to Bethlehem after all!"

"Good luck," said the carpenter.

"Haven't I seen you somewhere before?" Zach asked. There was something familiar about his face.

"I don't think so," said the carpenter. "Remember, follow that star!"

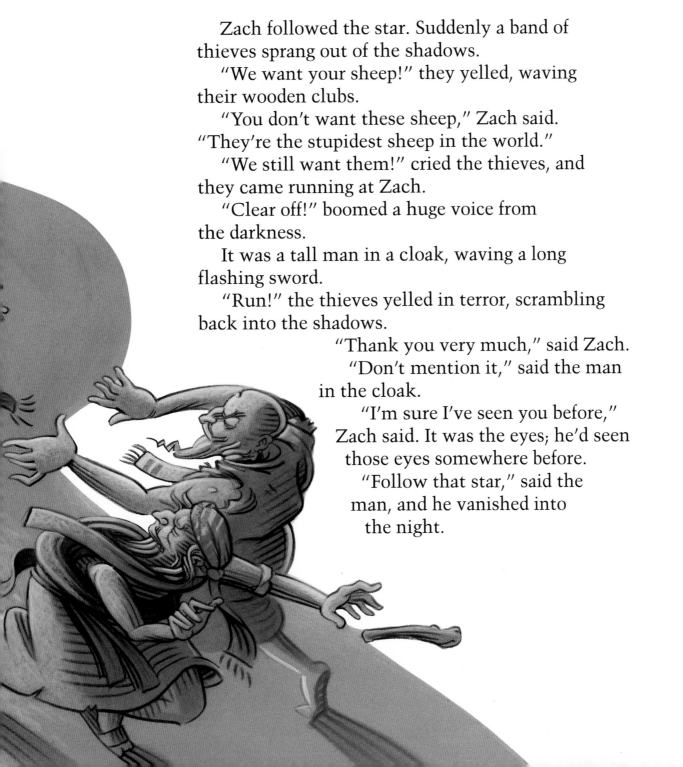

Zach followed the star. Suddenly a band of thieves sprang out of the shadows.

"We want your sheep!" they yelled, waving their wooden clubs.

"You don't want these sheep," Zach said. "They're the stupidest sheep in the world."

"We still want them!" cried the thieves, and they came running at Zach.

"Clear off!" boomed a huge voice from the darkness.

It was a tall man in a cloak, waving a long flashing sword.

"Run!" the thieves yelled in terror, scrambling back into the shadows.

"Thank you very much," said Zach.

"Don't mention it," said the man in the cloak.

"I'm sure I've seen you before," Zach said. It was the eyes; he'd seen those eyes somewhere before.

"Follow that star," said the man, and he vanished into the night.

Zach followed the star. It grew bigger and bigger.
He was sure he was almost there.

Then he came to a hill. It was so steep that the sheep kept falling down and tumbling back to the bottom. They lay there on their backs, bleating and baahing into the night sky.

Zach felt like crying. He sat down on a nearby sheep and clasped his head in his hands. He was never going to get to Bethlehem.

"Having sheep trouble?" a voice asked him.

It was a young boy in shabby clothes.

"My sheep can't get up the hill," Zach told him. "I'd carry them on my own back if I weren't so tired and there weren't so many of them."

"You need a slingshot," said the boy.

"What?" said Zach.

"We could rig a slingshot between these two trees and fire the sheep to the top of the hill! I've done this kind of thing before."

"It's worth a try," said Zach.

The boy stretched a long piece of leather between the trunks of two trees and pulled it back like a giant slingshot.

Zach shoved in the first sheep.

The boy let go and the sheep was catapulted through the air, bleating in confusion. It landed on all fours at the top of the hill.

"It works!" cried Zach.

One after another, they fired Zach's sheep up the hill.

From the hilltop, Zach could see the city of Bethlehem spread out before him.

"I made it," said Zach to the boy. "I couldn't have done it without you."

"Well," said the boy, "did you think we'd forget about you? The others sent me back to find you."

"Hey!" cried Zach. "I'm sure I've seen you somewhere before. You've got the same eyes as the old man, and the carpenter, and the man with the sword."

The boy shed his shabby clothes. He spread his wings and soared up into the sky, mist and light trailing from him. A wonderful smell filled the night air.

"You're an angel!" Zach exclaimed. "I've seen an angel!"

"That's nothing," laughed the angel. "Wait until you see what's in Bethlehem."

"You mean there's more?" asked Zach.

"Oh yes, much more," said the angel, his voice like wind chimes and oboes. "In a manger in a stable, you'll find what you've come all this way to see. It's something wonderful, something that's going to change the world!"

"How do I find the right stable?" Zach asked.

But he already knew the answer.

He looked up into the sky and saw the star.

All he had to do was follow it.

Luke 2: 8–14

And there were in the same country shepherds abiding in the field, keeping watch over their flock by night.

And, lo, the angel of the Lord came upon them, and the glory of the Lord shone round about them: and they were sore afraid.

And the angel said unto them, Fear not: for, behold, I bring you good tidings of great joy, which shall be to all people.

For unto you is born this day in the city of David a Saviour, which is Christ the Lord.

And this shall be a sign unto you; Ye shall find the babe wrapped in swaddling clothes, lying in a manger.

And suddenly there was with the angel a multitude of the heavenly host praising God, and saying,

Glory to God in the highest, and on earth peace, good will toward men.